THE MAKING OF TINTIN

HERGÉ

THE MAKING OF TINTIN

The Secret of the Unicorn
Red Rackham's Treasure
PLUS a full-colour section on how these two
Adventures came into being

by Benoit Peeters

English version by Leslie Lonsdale-Cooper

Methuen Children's Books · London

This edition first published in Great Britain
1983 by Methuen Children's Books
Michelin House, 81, Fulham Road, London SW3 6RB
Reprinted 1988
Copyright © 1982 by Carlsen If, Copenhagen
The Secret of the Unicorn, and
Red Rackham's Treasure copyright © 1947 by Casterman
English texts copyright © 1959 by
Methuen & Co Ltd
Postscript copyright © 1982 by Benoît Peeters
English version by Leslie Lonsdale-Cooper
copyright © 1983 by Methuen Children's Books Ltd
Printed by Casterman, S.A., Tournai, Belgium

ISBN 0 416 29300 X

THE SECRET OF THE UNICORN

NEWS IN BRIEF

AN alarming rise in the number of robberies has been reported in the past few weeks. Daring pickpockets are operating in the larger stores, the cinemas and street markets. A well-organised gang is believed to be at work. The police are using their best men to put a stop to this public scandal.

We must keep our eyes open, and catch these crooks.

How about starting in the Old Street Market? Tintin said he was going there this morning. Perhaps we'll meet him.

Good idea. Let's go.

Why, there are Thomson and Thompson.

Hello! ... How are you?

Look who's here!

Tintin!

What are you doing here? Looking for bargains?

Sh! ... Highly confidential! ... Special operation: pickpockets.

But that didn't stop us from finding this job-lot of walking sticks. ...

How much?

Eight bob for the lot.

Six shillings.

Seven ... but I'm robbin' meself ...

See? You've always got to haggle a bit, here.

My wallet's been stolen!

But that's absurd!... You must have left it at home.. or perhaps you've lost it?

No, I'm sure someone's stolen it!

Here, you hold these sticks. I'll pay.

Just the sort of thing that would happen to you!... To go and let someone pinch your wallet!

Mine's gone too!

Here. let me pay for them.

Thanks very much, Tintin. We'll pay you back tomorrow.

There.

Goodbye! We're going to report this straight away ...

Stop thief!... Help!... My suitcase!...

10

I'm sorry, sir, but this ship is not for sale.

Look, I'll give you a fiver for it!

A tenner!

NO!

Twenty!

Thirty!

Look here: I want to give this ship to a friend of mine. I'm not selling it, so please don't pester me any more!

Now why were they both so keen to buy my ship?

A few minutes later...

It really is superb... Captain Haddock will be delighted.

RRRING

I expect that's him...

I apologise: it's me again!

?

Forgive me if I am too insistent. But as I explained, I'm a collector - a collector of model ships. And I would be so very grateful if you would agree to sell me your ship.

I've already told you, I bought it for a friend...

Exactly! Now I have other ships just as good as yours, and we could exchange them so that your friend...

It's no good. Please don't go on. I'm keeping it.

Very well. But think it over. I'll give you my card, so that if you change your mind...

I shouldn't count on it!

Well, I shall hope.

Goodbye, sir.

CRASH

?

 What's happened ?

 Snowy !... What have you done ?

 Look, now it's broken !

 Luckily it's not too bad. I can soon mend it.

 RRRRING This time it must be the Captain.

 Hello ! Hello, Captain. Just the person I wanted to see.

 Come on in. I've got a surprise for you.

 Tintin, what a magnificent ship !

 Thundering typhoons !

 Where... where did you find this ship ? In the Old Street Market... Why ?

 Ten thousand thundering typhoons !... What a remarkable coincidence !... Imagine !...

 No ! Come with me : then you'll see !

 Remarkable !... It's really remarkable !

 Here we are! Now...

 You'll see...

 Look!

 Is... is that you?...

No, it's one of my ancestors, Sir Francis Haddock. He lived in the reign of Charles the Second.

But just take a closer look at that ship in the background...

 It's just like the one you saw in my room, isn't it?

Exactly!... It's the same ship!... It's identical!... Don't you think that's remarkable?

 There's a name here. Look there, in tiny letters: UNICORN

So there is: UNICORN. I'd never noticed it.

 Maybe there's a name on mine too... We should have brought it along. Wait here: I'll go and fetch it.

 If mine has the same name, that'll really be funny...

 Let's see...

 Great snakes!... It's gone!

RRRING...
RRRING...
RRRING...

Hello?... Yes... Ah, it's you... Well, has your ship got the same name?... What did you say?... It's been stolen?

Yes, stolen!... Do I suspect anybody? No one at all... at least... Look Captain, I'll ring you again later...

Yes... he's the only possibility...

IVAN IVANOVITCH SAKHARINE
Collector
21, Eucalyptus Avenue

Just you wait, Mr. Ivan Ivanovitch Sakharine!

Here we are...

EUCALYPTUS AVENUE

I've a hunch that we're off on one of our adventures again...

RRRING

21

Something tells me he's going to get a surprise when he opens the door!

Ah, there you are!... Come in... I was expecting you.

!

What?... Expecting me?... Then you know why I've come.

But of course...

You've come to tell me that you'll sell your ship after all...

Certainly not!

Not?... Then I don't understand...

Is this where you keep your collection?... I've come to tell you, sir... that my ship has been stolen...

... and that I'm waiting for you to explain how it comes to be here!

15

You are mistaken, young man. I've had this ship for more than ten years!...

Ten years? But you were trying to buy it from me less than two hours ago!

This wasn't the ship!... Not this one!... Yours was, in fact, exactly the same, but it wasn't this one!

Indeed?...

Well, sir, we can soon tell. Just after you'd gone, my ship fell over and the mainmast was broken. I put it back, but you can see where it broke. So we'll look at your mainmast, if you don't mind!

It's not broken!... This isn't my ship!

So, you see!

I can understand your surprise. I myself was amazed to find an exact replica of my own vessel in the Old Street Market. And because it seemed so odd, I did all I could to persuade you to part with it...

Please do forgive me, sir... I am so very sorry...

That's all right! And if you find your ship, let me know!

It's extremely odd! Two ships exactly like the one in the Captain's picture... and with the same name: UNICORN.

I must telephone the Captain at once: He'll be am-azed!

Engaged!

It really is unbelievable how long people can chatter on the telephone! More than a quarter of an hour! Ah, at last!

We can go now, Fifi: it has stopped raining...

!

No reply : the Captain must have gone out. We'll go home . . .

As for my burglar, it must have been the second man who tried to buy the ship . . .

My door's open ! . . . What can be the matter now ? . . .

My flat has been ransacked ! . . .

The gangsters ! What have they done to my books?

This one is completely ruined ! . . .
The vandals !

Burgled twice in one day . . .
Not bad at all !

What have they taken this time ?

Very queer thieves : they haven't taken a thing .

They've only searched the place . . . I wonder what they were looking for ? . . .

Next morning . . .

Hello. How are you?... Good heavens! Whatever's happened?

Er... nothing really ... just a little spot of bother, in the Old Street Market..

Er... yes... a slight mis-understanding. Anyway, we've come to pay you the money for those sticks. We called last night, but you were out.

Did you get your wallet back all right?

I'm afraid not. But I bought a new one this morning, and ... and...

Goodness gracious! I've been robbed again!

! !

Great Scotland Yard!... That man we met last night on the stairs, on our way here!... I remember now: he bumped into me!...

What was he like?

He bumped into me, too!

Quite tall... coarse features ... black hair... small black moustache... blue suit... brown hat...

That's him...the man from the Old Street Market!

But he couldn't have stolen your wallet last night, when you only bought it this morning.

There's something in what you say...

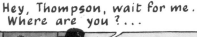

Miserable thieves! A brand new wallet! Come along, Thomson, we must report this right away!

He's right!... We must report it at once...

Look out!

Hey, Thompson, wait for me. Where are you?...

Here!... I'm downstairs already!

18

Poor old Thomsons, they do have rotten luck!... There seems to be quite an epidemic of larceny and house-breaking.

Oh well, let's try and get these papers sorted out...

What are you after, Snowy?

A cigarette, under there? That's a funny place...

Why, it's not a cigarette... it's a little scroll of parchment...

But this isn't mine! Where ever did it come from?... Let's have a closer look at it...

Here's another mystery!

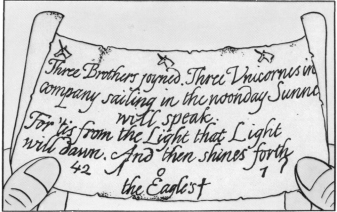

Three Brothers joyned. Three Unicornes in company sailing in the noonday Sunne will speak. For 'tis from the Light that Light will dawn. And then shines forth the Eagle's †
42   1

But it's all gibberish! And where on earth did this parchment come from, anyway?

Great snakes! I've got it... This parchment must have been rolled up inside the mast of the ship. It fell out when the mast was broken, and it rolled under the chest...

And that explains something else! ... Whoever stole my ship knew that the parchment was hidden there. When he discovered the scroll had gone, he thought I must have found it. That's why the thief came back and searched my flat, never guessing the parchment was under the chest...

Tintin, you're a real Sherlock Holmes!

But why was he so anxious to get hold of it? If only it made some sense... then at least...

I wonder... But... of course! ... That must be it! There's no other answer.

Quick, Snowy!... We must see the Captain.

Why? What is it now?

Treasure, Snowy!... Come on, this is going to be a treasure-hunt!

RRRING RRRING RRRING
HADDOCK

Yes, I'm absolutely certain it must be treas-ure...

The old lazybones! He's still in bed!
RRRING

No?... then where can he be?

No one at home. Perhaps he's gone out. I'll ask his land-lady...

Captain Haddock?... No, I didn't see him go out. Hasn't he answered the bell? That's funny..

Perhaps he's ill?

Ill? He might be... His light's been on all night...

We must find out at once.

RRRRRRRING

No answer?...

Wait!... He must be in. I can hear a noise...

20

Avast, pirates! Avast there!

Captain!...

Avast, you dogs!... Sea-gherkins!... Baboons!

Buccaneers!... Fili-busters!..Bagpipers!... Gallows-fodder!

We've won!... That's got them on the run! ...With a yo-ho-ho and a bottle of rum!

What's all this play-act-ing for?

Play-acting?...This isn't a play!... Come in, and you'll understand ...

You see that man?

Yes, he's one of your ancestors. What about it?

Well, last night, when I was thinking about this strange business of the ships, I suddenly remembered that up in the attic I had an old sea-chest belong-ing to my ancestor. This is it ...

In the chest I found this hat and cutlass, and also...

I know! Treasure!... Or a treasure-map!

No, not treasure, but something like it!... Old manuscripts by Sir Francis Haddock... Look, I started reading them yes-terday evening, and read all night...

Journal of Sir Francis Haddocke Captain in the King's Navy, Commander of the vessel Unicorn

I was still reading when you came in. That's why you found me a little... over-excited. But what a story! Just listen to it!

It is the year 1676. The UNICORN, a valiant ship of King Charles II's fleet, has left Barbados in the West Indies, and set sail for home. She carries a cargo of... well, anyway, there's a good deal of rum aboard...

Two days at sea, a good stiff breeze, and the UNICORN is reaching on the starboard tack. Suddenly there's a hail aloft...

Sail on the port bow!

Thundering typhoons!.. She's mighty close-hauled! Ration my rum if she's not going to cut across our bows!

And she's making a spanking pace! Oho! she's running up her colours.. Now we'll see...

!

The Jolly Roger! Pirates!...

Ahoy there!... Clear the decks for action!... Man the poop!.. Stand by to haul the wind!

Turning on to the wind with all sails set, risking her masts, the UNICORN tries to outsail the dreaded Barbary buccaneers ...

Thundering typhoons! It's no use... She's overhauling us fast!

They must outwit the pirates. The Captain makes a daring plan. He'll wear ship, then pay off on the port tack. As the UNICORN comes abreast of the pirate he'll loose off a broadside... No sooner said than done!...

Ready about!... Let go braces!... Beat gunners to quarters!

The UNICORN has gybed completely round. Taken by surprise, the pirates have no time to alter course. The royal ship bears down upon them... Steady...

FIRE!

Got her!

Got her, yes! But not a crip-pling blow. The pirate ship in turn goes about - and look! she's hoisted fresh colours to the mast-head!

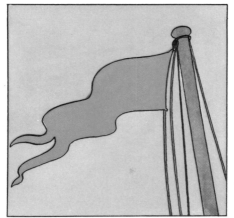

The red pennant!... No quarter given!... A fight to the death, no prisoners taken! You under-stand? If we're beaten, then it's every man to Davy Jones's locker!

The pirates take up the chase - they draw closer... and closer... Throats are dry aboard the UNICORN.

Close hauled, the enemy falls in line astern with UNICORN, avoiding the fire of her guns ... She draws closer...

Then suddenly, not more than half a cable's length away, she slips from under the UNICORN's poop...whoosh, like that!

Then she resumes her course. The two ships are now along-side. The boarders prepare for action ...

Here they come! Grappling irons are hurled from the enemy ship. With hideous yells the pirates stream aboard the UNICORN.

All hands to repel boarders!

Sir Francis?... When he came round he found himself securely lashed to his own mast. He suffered terribly...

From that blow on the head, of course...

No, from thirst!...

Poor man, how he suffered.

He looked about him. The deck was scrubbed, and no trace remained of the fearful combat that had taken place there. The pirates passed to and fro, each with a different load...

What's happening? Instead of pillaging our ship and making off with the booty, they're doing just the opposite.

But there's a man approaching. He wears a crimson cloak, embroidered with a skull: he's the pirate chief! He comes near - his breath reeks of rum - and he says:

Regard me well, dog: I am Red Rackham!

Your servant, sir. And I am Sir Francis Haddock.

Doesn't my name freeze your blood, eh? Right. Listen to me. You have killed Diego the Dreadful, my trusty mate. More than half my crew are dead or wounded. My ship is foundering; damaged by your first attack, then holed below the waterline as we boarded you...

...when some of your dastardly gunners fired at point blank range. She's sinking...so my men are transferring to this ship the booty we captured from a Spaniard three days ago.

And what booty!

Look at these diamonds!

29

These are worth more than six times a king's ransom...

Did you come here just to tell me that?

No, that's not why I came. I came to tell you that those who annoy me pay dearly for their folly! Tomorrow morning I shall hand you over to my crew. And that flock of lambs know just how to administering a lingering death!

So saying, he laughed sardonically, picked up his glass and drained it at a gulp, like this...

That's enough, Captain! Go on with your story...

Very well. Towards nightfall, the UNICORN with her pirate crew sighted a small island. Soon she dropped anchor in a sheltered cove...

Darkness fell; the pirates found the UNICORN's cargo of rum, broached the casks, and made themselves abominably drunk...

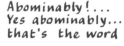

Abominably!... Yes abominably... that's the word...

Hey, what's the idea?... I only wanted to show you...

You don't have to, I quite understand.

Just as you like, Tintin... Now where was I?

The pirates were abominably drunk...

AAAAA-AAAAH!

That's funny! Now there are two glasses!

Well, in the meantime...

In the meantime Sir Francis struggled desperately to free himself...

Just you wait, my lambkins! Ration my rum if Sir Francis Haddock doesn't soon give you something to remember him by...

Done it! That's one hand free!

Free! Now I'm free!

On your guard, Red Rackham: here I come!

And with these words he hurled himself...

On the pirates?.. Like that?... Unarmed?...

No, on a bottle of rum, rolling on the deck!... He opened it, put it to his lips, and...

And then he stops. "This is no time for drinking," he says, "I need all my wits about me". With that, he puts down the bottle...

Yes, he puts down the bottle... and seizes a cutlass. Then, looking towards the fo'c'sle where the drunken roistering still goes on...

You sing and carouse, little lambs!... I'm off to the magazine!

You know, of course, the magazine in a ship is where they store the gunpowder and shot...

There!... The party won't be complete without some fireworks!

Now I must make haste! There's just time for me to leave the ship before she goes up!

So, I've caught you!

!

So, dog, high!... Well, I'll be— you'd blow us sky-... that pleasure! Well, you won't skin you alive, fore I even douse that fuse!

By Lucifer! I'll shave your beard, porcupine!

And I'll pluck those feathers, squawking popinjay! Fancy-dress freebooter! fresh water pirate! Pithecanthropus!

Retreat as you may, you cannot escape me!

I'll run you through, prattling porpoise!

And as he fought, Sir Francis kept thinking of that fuse, about to touch off the powder at any moment...

Suddenly, nimbly parrying a thrust, he leapt to one side...

With one swift blow from his heel he extinguished the fuse!

WOOOAH!

Now, Red Rackham, my temper's rising!

BANG
THUMP
ZZINNG
CRACK

Victory! Red Rackham lies dead! With a yo-ho-ho and a bottle of rum!

That's that! May heaven forgive your wicked soul!

Enough delay! Now to light another fuse...

...and be off!

No one has seen me: they're still drinking. Quick, into the jolly-boat...

Jusht look at the j-jolly-boat... Ish...ish going away...

Nonshensh! You're sheeing shings... you'sh drunk...

Hurrah! Justice is done!

So perished the UNICORN, that stout ship commanded by Sir Francis Haddock. And of all the pirates aboard her, not one escaped with his life...

What happened to Sir Francis after that?

He made friends with the natives on the island, and lived among them for two years. Then he was picked up by a ship which carried him back home. There his journal ends. But now comes the strangest thing in the whole story ...

On the last page of the manuscript there is a sort of Will, in which he bequeaths to each of his three sons a model - built and rigged by himself - a model of the very ship he once blew up rather than leave her to the pirates. There's one funny detail: he tells his sons to move the mainmast slightly aft on each model. "Thus," he concludes, "the truth will out".

That's it, Captain!... Red Rackham's treasure will be ours!

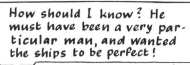
What do you mean?

Why do you suppose Sir Francis told his sons to move the mainmast on each of the three ships?

How should I know? He must have been a very particular man, and wanted the ships to be perfect!

In that case, he would have moved the masts himself. Why did he tell his sons to do it?

Because if his sons had obeyed him, they would have found a tiny scroll of parchment inside each mast!

What's that? How do you know?

Because I myself found the parchment hidden in the ship I bought in the Old Street Market. Here it is...

My wallet!... Someone's stolen my wallet...

Stolen it? You've probably left it at home.

No, it's been stolen. It was taken in the bus, on my way here. I remember being jostled...

What was on the parchment?

Wait... er... yes: *Three brothers joyned* - that's the three sons. *Three Vnicorns in company sailing in the noonday Sunne will speak* - that means we must get the three ships to deliver their secret: the three parchments. The rest... isn't so easy...

For 'tis from light that light will dawn. And then shines forth ... and then some numbers, and at the end, a little cross follows the words *the Eagle's*... that's all.

But what can it mean?

I don't know yet, but I'm sure that if we can collect the three scrolls together, then we shall find Red Rackham's diamonds. I already know where the second one is. Come on, Captain!

You know where the second scroll is?

Yes, I know who's got the second UNICORN.

The second UNICORN built by my ancestor?

Yes, it belongs to a certain Mr. Sak- harine.

This is it: he lives here, at Number 21.

HELP!.. HELP!.. HELP!...

What's the matter? OOOH!...

Ooooh! Lord love us! It's Mr. Sakharine... Someone's murdered Mr. Sakharine!...

?

Dead?

No, he's alive: his heart's beating. He's been chloroformed...

Tintin, look there! The second UNICORN... and the mast's broken!

Look! The foot of the mast is hollow: the parchment has gone!

Thundering typhoons! We aren't the only ones hunting for Red Rackham's treasure!

Don't move, anyone!

Ah, my old friends! I...

I'm sorry. We're on duty. On duty we can have no friends!

Quite right! We're here to clear up this business...

First, here's the victim...

To be precise: here's the victim!

Now, if there's a victim, there must be a culprit.

A brilliant deduction! Now we only have to find him... and he can't be far away. To be precise: he isn't far away...

In fact, there he is!

Me, the culprit? You dare accuse me?... Miserable earth-worms!.. Sea-gherkins!

Slave-traders!.. Sea-lice! ...Black-beetles!...Baboons!

Artichokes!...Vermicellis!... Phylloxera!... Pyrographers!

Crab-apples!... Goosecaps!... Gogglers!... Jelly-fish!

Captain! Captain! Calm yourself!

Yes, please calm yourself, Captain. We only said that by way of an experiment...

What sort of experiment?

You see, if you really had been guilty, you'd have been upset. As it is, we are now quite convinced of your innocence.

Now, to work! We must look for fingerprints.

Goodness gracious!...The corpse has gone!

Look!...Your corpse is coming round!

What happened to you, Mr Sakharine?

A man came here last night, to offer me some fine old engravings. As I bent over to look at them I felt a pad clamped over my nose...

No doubt it was chloroform, for I became unconscious...

Very odd...To be precise... Can you smell something burning?

Your magnifying-glass! Ha! ha! ha!... your magnifying-glass... and the sun!... Ha! ha! ha!..

Stop laughing in that stupid way! Try to concentrate on the case.

Can you describe the man who came to offer you those engravings?

Wait... I seem to have seen him before... but I can't tell where...

He was rather fat. Black hair, and a little black moustache. He wore a blue suit, and a brown hat.

That's him!... That's the man in the Old Street Market!

What man in the Old Street Market!

A man who tried to buy the ship I found in the Old Street Market. You know him too: he's the one you met on the stairs on your way to see me last night. You suspected him of stealing your wallet...

By the way, do you know mine has been stolen too?...

No! It's extraordinary how many people let their wallets be stolen! It's so easy not to... Here, you try and take mine...

Go on, try!...

It's on elastic!

Simple enough... If you only think of it!

Childishly simple, in fact. But now we must leave you to your investigations. Goodbye...

Goodbye.

If things go on like this, Red Rackham's treasure will disappear from under our noses...

Yes, I'm afraid so...

Look, someone seems to be waiting for us outside my door...

The man from the Old Street Market!

Mr. Tintin?...

Next morning...

SHOOTING DRAMA

AN unknown man was shot dead in Labrador Road just before midday yesterday. As he was about to enter No. 26, three shots were fired from a passing car which had slowed down opposite him. The victim was struck by all three bullets in the region of the heart. He died without regaining consciousness.

Poor devil. No one will ever know what he meant when he pointed to those sparrows.

Hello, Captain! Come in... I'm just telephoning the hospital for news of the wounded man...

It's no good: he's dead.

Hello?... Is that the House-Surgeon? This is Tintin... Good-morning, Doctor. How's our injured man? Just the same? Still unconscious?... Is there any hope? A little... yes... Thank you. Goodbye.

But look here: it says in the paper that he's dead.

Yes, the papers were told he'd died. The crooks will believe he didn't give them away, so they won't be on their guard, and they'll get caught one day.

Ah, I see now. But I still wonder what that poor chap meant, pointing at those sparrows...

So do I, Captain. It's all very mysterious. "To be precise: very mysterious", as the Thomsons would say.

Another day watching for pickpockets all over the place. I'll be glad to get back home.

Here comes our bus at last!

My wallet!... This time I've got you, you scoundrel!

Stop, villain!

40

Ah, Captain!... Come with me...

Where?..

To see the Thomsons: they've found my wallet!

There's no mistake: it's mine all right.

He had seven in his pockets. The day's takings, no doubt.

?

Here's the parchment from the UNICORN's mast. Look, Captain...

Er... that's good...

Tell me: how did you manage to catch the thief?

Catch him?... Well, to be quite honest, we only managed to catch his morning-coat.

Yes, it's certainly a morning-coat. How odd for a pickpocket to wear a thing like this.

Isn't it?

The trouble is that the coat doesn't give us any clue about its owner's identity...

Doesn't it?

Look at these stitches; they make up a number. That means the coat has been to the cleaners recently.

Goodness, you're right!

So... to find the thief's name and address, we've only got to trace the cleaners who use this mark. Quick, we'll make a list of cleaners from the telephone directory, and start hunting for the thief at once!

Some days later ...

Mr. Tintin ?

The first floor.

All right ?

O.K., O.K.

Mr. Tintin ? Here's the dinner service you ordered.

Me ? I haven't ordered anything.

But it's addressed to you ... Look ...

Right! the chloroform's done the trick. Quick, shove him in the crate.

Wait: I'll shut the door.

?

WOOAH! WOOAH!

Wasn't Mr. Tintin in ?

Yes, but there's some mistake. He hadn't ordered anything.

That confounded tyke's at the window!

?

WOOAH! WOOAH!

Hello, Snowy! What's the matter ?

43

Nobody there! But I wasn't dreaming: someone spoke!

Yes, someone spoke!

Who... who are you?... And where are you?

Who am I? I am the ghost of the captain of the UNICORN!

Ha! ha! ha! ha! ha!

Ha! ha! ha!... That frightened you, didn't it?... Come over to the door... Come on.

Come nearer. Good... Now, can you see the speaking-tube?

Who are you, and what do you want with me?

Who am I?... You must allow me to remain anonymous... And why did I have you kidnapped? You have guessed that, no doubt...

I want to know where you have hidden the two parchments you stole from me.

Me? I stole two parchments?... But I never had more than one.

Come on now, let's be sensible! I'd collected two of the three scrolls: you took them from me. That night when I had your flat searched, only the third one was found... in your wallet. Where are the other two!

How should I know?

As you like. But I warn you: I know of several ways to loosen stubborn tongues... I'll give you two hours to tell me where you hid those scrolls, then if you won't talk, you'll soon see the sort of man I am!

But I tell you... Oh he's cut off, the gangster!

Now I'm in a fine mess! How do I get out of this one?

SPLOSH

Two hours!... Two hours to get out of here!... How can I do it?

?

I wonder if I could use this beam as a battering-ram, against the door...

Hopeless! I can hardly lift it...

No good. But in two hours I must be miles away...

!

Eureka!

First I'd better block up this speaking tube with my handkerchief

Then no one will hear any noise I may make...

Now to work! As fast as I can...

First I'll knot these sheets and blankets together...

Then tie them securely to this beam...

And pull!... Heave-ho!... Heave-ho!... Heave-ho!... Heave!...

Start again: I've simply got to move this beam. Now...

Meanwhile...

!

A quick bath and I'll soon get rid of this mud.

Aha! It's good to be nice and clean again.

That's it: there's the beam under the ring.

Now I'll tie a small stone to the end of this string, like this ...

Whoops!

And that's made a fine battering-ram!

Now then, here we go!

WHAM

Did you hear that?

Yes, a muffled thud. It shook the whole house.

There it is again...

That's odd...Sounded as if it came from the cellars...

BOOM

From the cellars? But...

By thunder! It must be Tintin. I expect he's calling us - to tell us where those scrolls are hidden...

Hello?... Hello Tintin?... Hello?... Hello?...That's funny: he's not answering ...

But the noise is going on.

We must get to the bottom of this. Come with me; we'll see what's happening.

BOOM

Whew! I just saved it in time!

BOOM

This time it's Tintin... We've got him now.

He can't be far off...

There he is!... Stop!... Stop!... or I'll shoot!

BANG
BANG

A counting-frame!... that gives me an idea...

CRACK

That was a good idea . . .

Little devil! He'll pay dearly for this . . .

So sorry to have to leave you, gentlemen . . .

And now, tough guys, it's your turn to be locked in . . .

No time to lose. I must have these gangsters arrested at once.

!

Steady... they're coming!

This way out!

The front door just slammed. Get up, you two. He'll escape us...

Free at last!

There he goes!

Crumbs, they're after me again!

Missed! He's disappeared among the trees!

Fetch Brutus, Nestor! Quickly!

Brutus? Very well, sir!

What an enormous park: it's like a forest...

WOOF! WOOF!

Find him, Brutus! Find him!

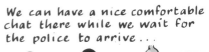

59

Where are they going? ... Oh, I see: that little wretch is taking care to put Brutus back in his kennel.

WOOF! WOOF!

That's that! And now, gentlemen, we'll go to the police-station!

They're coming back this way: they'll pass under the ground-floor windows. Perhaps there's some way...

Keep cool, Nestor!

Here they come! Careful, don't miss...

Nestor!

Oh, dear, I didn't hit him hard enough...

Now then, once more...

Oh dear!!

Got you this time, my young friend!

60

That's one for you, sycophant!

That thug had come round - he was just going shoot you ...

Let me go!... I keep telling you - it's all a mistake: I'm not the one to arrest...

Ah, here come Thomson and Thompson... Hello.

It's this little ruffian, this little wretch who broke into the house and terrorized my masters; he's a real gangster, Mr. Detective...

It's true, Nestor acted in good faith. I heard his master say I was a criminal. Nestor believed it.

Then your masters are the criminals. Look what's left of my bottle of three-star brandy! It's all their fault!... They're gangsters!... dizzards!.. baboons!

And what's more, we have a warrant for their arrest.

My wallet! My wallet! It's incredible!

But your wallet's there...

That's just what's incredible: no one has stolen it!

By the way, what about that pickpocket?... Have you managed to lay hands on him?

Not yet, but it won't be long now. ..

We got his name from the Stellar Cleaners: he's called Aristides Silk. We were just about to pull him in when we were ordered to arrest the Bird brothers, and here we are...

Quiet! Quiet! Listen to me!

Gentlemen, there has been a miscarriage of justice! This man is innocent, as Tintin said. Won't you take off these handcuffs... and let him go and fetch me another bottle of brandy?

There, my man, now you're free. And we'll use these handcuffs for your masters!

We'll follow you, Nestor. Don't forget; it's to be three-star!

Now, Captain, tell me how you came to be here.

Oh, yes... Right. Well...

Just after your telephone call — and I didn't und— erstand a word of that — someone rang up from the hospital...

...where they still had the little-birds-man. After hovering between life and death, he'd just come round and identified his attackers: the Bird brothers, antique dealers of Marlinspike Hall. It was only when I heard that name...

...that I understood what you meant on the telephone. There was no time to lose: I warned the police at once, and we rushed here...

WHAM * OH!
WHAM OW!

?   ?

We shouldn't have left the police with those two gangsters!...

Look!... one's escaping!... there! He's just turned the corner!

He's the most dangerous of the two: he mustn't get away!

BRRRR BRRR

A car! That's a car starting up!

Barnaby came back empty-handed. Then he suddenly remembered the other man who'd been trying to buy the ship from you.

And next day he visited Mr. Sakharine, chloroformed him, and stole the third parchment...

That's right. But after he'd given it to us, he and Max quarrelled violently about the money we'd agreed he should have. Barnaby demanded more, but Max stuck to the original sum. Finally Barnaby went, furiously angry and saying we'd regret our meanness. When he'd gone, Max got cold feet: supposing the wretch betrayed us? We jumped into the car and trailed him; our fears were justified. We saw him speaking...

... to you. Panicking in case he'd given the whole game away, Max caught up with you in a few seconds, and shot Barnaby as he stepped into your doorway.

I understand so far: but tell me, why did you kidnap me?

We told you: to make you give up the two parchments you had stolen from us a few days after the shooting.

I see. But I couldn't have stolen them as I didn't know you existed! But I wonder... Perhaps it was...

Yes, perhaps it was Mr. Sakharine who took the two scrolls?

Hurrah! That's it!

At last! ...He's managed to get it off for me...

Come on, Captain, we'd better help this poor chap...

Ready! Steady! He-e-eave!

Whoops!

Captain, as soon as we return we'll see Mr. Sakharine. I'm sure he took the two scrolls...

Yes, we've only got one...

One! Great snakes! we haven't even got that! The Bird brothers took it! But we can get it back!

Give me back the parchment you stole from my room!

Give it back?... That's impossible... Max has it in his pocket!

!

Ring up the police station at once; give them a description of Max Bird, and his car number - LX188. Then we'll go straight back to town...

Right!

Next morning...

Now for Mr. Sakharine...

RRRING

Mr Sakharine! He's gone away, young man. He won't be back for a fortnight

He would be away! That doesn't make things any easier!

In the meantime I'll go and see the Thomsons. Perhaps they'll be able to tell me if they've found Max Bird...

Good morning. Are you going out?... I just came to ask you...

Sh! Mum's the word! Come with us!

Where are we going?

You'll soon see...

...and a few minutes later...

RAT TAT TAT TAT

66

Mr. Aristides Silk?

Yes...

I arrest you in the name of the law!

Arrest me?...

Yes, you! You are a thief, sir!...

A thief! Aristides Silk, retired civil servant: a thief! It's a mistake, gentlemen, a shocking mistake!

I'm sorry to interrupt you, Mr. Silk, but could you explain the meaning of all this?...

I...er, yes... Well, I... you see, I'm not a thief: certainly not! But I'm a bit of a... kleptomaniac. It's something stronger than I am: I adore wallets. So I... I... just find one from time to time. I put a label on it, with the owner's name

... and I add it to my collection ...

I venture to say, gentlemen, that this is a unique collection of its kind. And when I tell you that it only took me three months to assemble you'll agree that it's a remarkable achievement ...

It's amazing! All these wallets in alphabetical order ...

I wonder if by some extraordinary coincidence ...

Hooray!

Property of Max Bird pinched on 1 - 5 - 58

And here are the two pieces of parchment!... Captain, Red Rackham's treasure is ours!

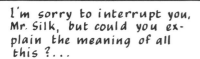

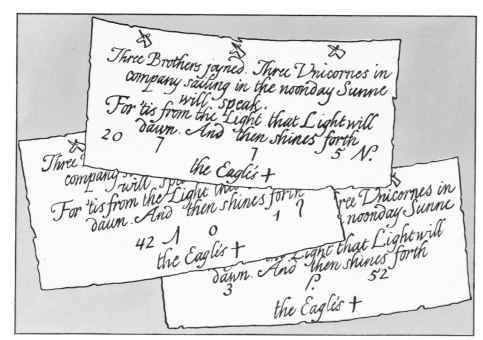

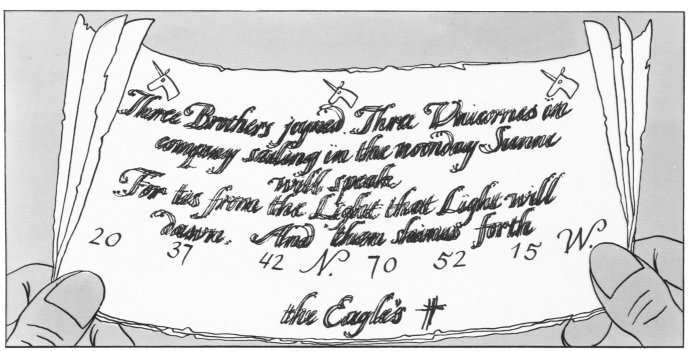

A latitude and a longitude!

Obviously telling us where the UNICORN sank!

Now, Captain... When do we leave on our treasure-hunt?

When do we leave? ... Er...

Let's see... First we need a ship... We can charter the SIRIUS, a trawler belonging to my friend, Captain Chester... Then we need a crew, some diving suits and all the right equipment for this sort of expedition... That will take us a little time to arrange. We'd better say a month. Yes, in a month we could be ready to leave.

Red Rackham's treasure will be ours!

But of course it won't be easy, and we shall certainly have plenty of adventures on our treasure-hunt... You can read about them in RED RACKHAM'S TREASURE

- HERGÉ -

RED RACKHAM'S *TREASURE*

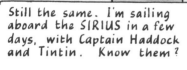

¹ See The Secret of the Unicorn

Red Rackham's Treasure

THE forthcoming departure of the trawler *Sirius* is arousing speculation in sea-faring circles. Despite the close secrecy which is being maintained, our correspondent understands that the object of the voyage is nothing less than a search for treasure.

This treasure, once the hoard of the pirate Red Rackham, lies in the ship *Unicorn*, sunk at the end of the seventeenth century. Tintin, the famous reporter—whose sensational intervention in the Bird case made headline news—and his friend Captain Haddock, have discovered the exact resting-place of the *Unicorn*,

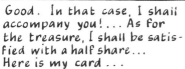

RED RACKHAM

There you are. That's got rid of that gang of thieves!

RRRRING

Another?

Wait, I'll go . . .

Is that you Tintin? . . . It's us, Thomson and Thompson. Could you give us a hand? . . . A wild elephant dropped something on our heads.

!

Come in; we'll see to that . . .

RRRING

?

I'd like to speak to Mr. Tintin.

Why? . . . No doubt your name happens to be Red Rackham?

Yes?

No, I'm asking you if you're called Red Rackham . . .

Oh?

WHAT'S YOUR NAME?

Please speak a bit louder. I'm a little hard of hearing.

YOUR NAME!

Gone away? . . . What a pity! Never mind, I'll come again. I particularly wanted to speak to Mr. Tintin himself. . . .

I'm Tintin. What do you want?

Ah, Mr. Tintin! . . . They told me that you were away.

I'm delighted to meet you. My name is Calculus; Cuthbert Calculus.

Oh?

No, Calculus, Cuthbert Calculus. Mr. Tintin, I understand you are setting off on a search for treasure. That's nice. But have you considered the sharks?

The sharks?

No, young man, I'm talking about the sharks. I expect you intend to do some diving. In which case, beware of sharks!

But...

Don't you agree?... But I've invented a machine for underwater exploration, and it's shark-proof. If you'll come to my house with me, I'll show it to you.

I'm very sorry but...

No, it's not far. Less than ten minutes...

I'm afraid I'm very busy and I...

Why of course. Certainly these gentlemen may come too.

It's no good. There's no time! NO TIME!

Good, that's settled. We'll go at once.

I'm so glad you agreed to come!

Please don't mention it.

No. Calculus, Cuthbert Calculus.

You see, here we are. One more floor...

It's in here...

Yes, that's a new device for putting bubbles in soda-water...

And that's a clothes-brushing machine.

Not a bad gadget, eh?

76

No, Professor Calculus, I said your machine won't do for us!

Oh, good!

Well, gentlemen, that's agreed. I'll make another smaller one. It will be ready in eight days' time...

Well, we're all ready to start - at least, if we can find a diving-suit. I've spent three days hunting through marine stores, and I still haven't unearthed one.

I say, look there!

Great snakes! Let's go and see...

FOR SALE
Complete Diving Equipment, as new

We'd like to see the diving equipment, please.

The diving-suit? Please follow me.

There ...

Beware, young fellow, beware! Money is the root of all evil!

?

Why... why do you say that?

Why?... Because I see that you intend to go treasure-hunting ...

You see that? Where can you see it?

I read it in your face.

In my face?... But... but ... what's unusual about my face? Tintin, can you see anything?

Well, I...

Blistering barnacles!

It's horrible!... What's happened to me? ...

Nothing, Captain! It's just that you were looking in a concave mirror! And here's a convex one!

Thank goodness!

But here's another mirror...I'll just reassure myself!

Oh!

Seven years of bad luck!

And two pounds for the mirror!

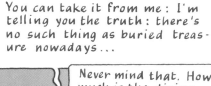

You can take it from me: I'm telling you the truth: there's no such thing as buried treasure nowadays...

Never mind that. How much is the diving-suit?

Ten pounds.

All right. We'll have it collected this afternoon. Shall we go, Captain?

Remember what I said, my lad. You won't find any treasure!

Next day...

SIRIUS

Good morning, Captain. All well?

No, bad!

Yes, bad. Very bad...I'm ill... 'Flu, I expect...And I've been thinking...I...well... briefly, to put it in a nutshell, I'm not going!

!

You can't be serious!

Perfectly serious. I'm not superstitious, but to break a mirror on the eve of a voyage... No, definitely, I'm not going!

Hello!

Bad news, my friends. We've just heard that Max Bird has escaped!

What did I tell you?... A good start, isn't it? ...

Yes, that troublesome antique dealer—he managed to give two policemen the slip when he was being taken for questioning.

That's bad...

There's a letter for you, Captain.

For me?...What's this about?

Billions of bilious blue blistering barnacles!

Is it bad news, Captain?

Read for yourself! It's ghastly!

DOCTOR A. LEECH

Dear Captain,
  I have considered your case, and conclude that your illness is due to poor liver condition.
You must therefore undergo the following treatment:
DIET – STRICTLY FORBIDDEN:
All alcoholic beverages (wine, beer, cider, spirits, cocktails

Good-day, gentlemen! I hope I'm not intruding?

No? Well, I'm happy to tell you my machine is ready now. When may I come aboard?

You can't come aboard! We aren't interested in your machine!

Tomorrow?

No not tomorrow! Never!

Today?... Good. I'll go and fetch it at once.

At last we are on our way, Snowy.

Tintin!

A radio message...

"Port Commander to Captain SIRIUS. Reduce speed. Motor boat coming out to you."

What can this mean?

Look!... There's a motor-boat coming now.

I can't quite see the passenger; but it'd better not be Professor Calculus!

Thomson and Thompson! What are they coming aboard for?

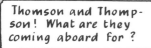

Hello! We're coming with you!

Coming with us?...

Yes, we've had orders to protect you.

Protect us? Is someone threatening us?...

Yes, you are in danger. Max Bird, the antique dealer, was seen last night skulking near the SIRIUS. He may try to take his revenge.

Just let him try! He'll find out...

Maybe, maybe. But anyway, now we are aboard you will be able to feel that you are perfectly safe.

To be precise: perfectly safe.

We shall see... Meanwhile we must find you a berth. Let's see... We've a couple of spare bunks for'ard. Will that do?

Yes, thanks!

Captain!... Captain!

Captain, I can't stand it!

What?

This thieving Snowy- he's stolen a whole box of biscuits!

No?...

Snowy?...

Yes, Snowy! I saw him just now near the galley!

Snowy!... Where is the wretched animal?

Snowy?... SNOWY?...

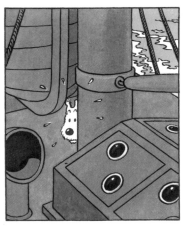

I can't see him, the scoundrel! But don't worry, I'll see that it doesn't happen again...

Good.

Er... our cabin is for'ard, isn't it?

Yes, for'ard.

We'll change at once, and mix discreetly with the ship's company...

Good idea!

We must behave like old sea-dogs ...

For a start, we'd better learn to chew tobacco. All old sea-dogs chew a quid. Here, have one of these...

What do we do, Captain? We're bearing down on that fishing fleet...

Give a blast on the siren; that'll warn them.

TOOOOOT

Goodness!... My tobacco!..

Mine... mine too ... I swallowed it!...

Next day ...

This has got to stop!...
Yes, it's got to stop!

Yes, Captain. Yesterday it was a box of biscuits! This morning a whole chicken has disappeared!

The wretched dog!

Snowy!...
Snowy!...
Where's he hiding?...
Snowy!

Snowy!... Snowy!...

What's the matter, Captain?

The matter?. Blistering barnacles, my bottle of whisky has vanished!

Vanished? Someone must be worried about your health and is keeping you to your diet...

You can laugh! ...But if I catch the crook, he's in for a rough time!

We'll investigate it in the morning. Now let's go to bed. I'm dead tired. Good night!

You go to sleep if you like. I know what I'm going to do

Thundering typhoons!

THUMP THUMP THUMP

Tintin, Tintin, come quickly!... There's not a moment to lose!...

We're going to blow up!... There's a bomb in the hold!...

I went down to the hold to open a case of whisky. And instead of whisky I found a bomb there!...

Here we are... Careful!

In here... Look...

Careful!... Don't go near it!

I must. We've got to get to the bottom of this...

Well?...

Steel plates!

Steel plates?...

You're right, by thunder!... Then it's not a bomb after all?...

Definitely not. Look, we'll open another case...

Blistering barnacles! More steel plates!

And in this one...

More steel plates!

Steaming blood! There's not a drop of whisky aboard! If I catch the monster who played this trick on us, he'll be in for a rough time!...

Come on, Captain. We'll try and solve this mystery in the morning...

Next day...

Anyway, we can't accuse Snowy any more. Some biscuits, even a chicken perhaps. But not a bottle of whisky!

OH!

Great snakes!... He...he... why, he's drunk!

Snowy, what have you done? Pooh! Your breath smells of whisky!

Now come on!... Show us where you found the whisky...

All right... You...you want a d-d-d-drink too?

? ?

Look!

See, the bottle must have smashed up there. Let's investigate.

There!

Blistering barnacles! If I ever catch him!

Sh!... Listen...

ZZZ...ZZZ... ZZZ...

Someone is asleep in this life-boat!

Impossible: the lashings are secure ...At least...

Blistering barnacles! The lashings are free this side! There's someone in this life-boat!

Thundering typhoons!

ZZZ... ZZZ ...ZZZ...

BISCUITS

Billions of bilious blue blistering barnacles! Get up, you!...

My whisky, you wretch!... What have you done with my whisky? Thundering typhoons, answer me!... Where's my whisky?

I must confess, I did sleep rather badly. But I hope you will give me a cabin...

A cabin!... I'll give you a cabin!.. I'm going to stow you in the bottom of the hold for the rest of the voyage, on dry bread and water!... And my whisky?... Where's my whisky?

It's on board, of course!

It's on board!... Heaven be praised!

Naturally it is in separate pieces...

In separate pieces... My whisky is in separate pieces?

Of course, it is a little smaller than the first one, but nevertheless it was too big to pass unnoticed. So I had to dismantle it and pack all the parts in the cases...

But what about the whisky out of those cases! Tell me! Is it still ashore?...

Oh no!

No, no. It was the night before you sailed. The cases were still on the quay, ready to be embarked. I took out all the bottles they contained, and put the pieces of my machine in their place...

Wretch!...Ignoramus! ...Abominable Snowman! ...I'll throw you overboard! Overboard, d'you hear?...

Thank you, Captain, thank you very much! It's just what I expected from you... Such a kind welcome! You'll see – you won't regret it.

Some days later...

Look. We have reached the position indicated by the parchments. We should soon see the island off which the UNICORN sank...

Isn't the island marked on any charts?

No, but that sometimes happens with small, unimportant islands. Come on, we'll try to spot it...

I can't see anything yet... Can you?...

Nothing.

Can you see anything?...

Not yet. But there's a bottle of champagne for the first one to sight land!

Over there!

Where's the island?... I can't see anything...

It was, Captain A shark, I know it was! I saw one, I really did!

Still no sign... It's very strange...

What's the name of the island?

How should I know?... It's not marked on any of the charts.

Oh?... But you are sure we're near it?

Positive! I plotted the position yesterday at noon.

Yes, I see. But... er... supposing you made a mistake in your calculations...

!

Oh, so I made a mistake in my calculations, did I?... All right: they're on my table. Go and check them!... Yes, you! Now! Go on! Check them!

Tell me, Captain, was that a fish jumping out of the water just now?

No, it was a grand piano!

Ah, I didn't think it could have been a fish...

A few minutes later...

You must forgive me, Captain, but there really is a little mistake in your calculations. Look, this is where we are, exactly...

You are right... I have made a mistake Gentlemen, please take off your hats...

Why must we take off our hats, Captain?...

Sh!...

? ?

Now...

But Captain, tell us what you mean...

I mean, gentlemen, that according to your calculations we are now standing inside Westminster Abbey!

Thousands of thundering typhoons! Where's that miserable island got to?

I'm beginning to think Sir Francis Haddock was pulling our legs.

I'm beginning to think so too!

We'll soon see! It's almost noon. We'll take a sight. I'll go and fetch my sextant.

That's it... Let's go in, and I'll work it out...

The figures given in the parchments were latitude 20° 37' 42" North, longitude 70° 52' 15" West. Here's our position now; the same latitude, longitude 71° 2' 29" West.

So we've already passed the right point, and yet we saw nothing... I simply can't understand it!

Captain, I think I've got it!

!

What do you mean?

Well, the meridian from which you calculated the degrees of longitude was of course the Greenwich meridian...

You don't suppose I used one in Timbuctoo!

No, wait. Supposing Sir Francis Haddock used a French chart — he easily could have done. Then zero would be on the Paris meridian — and that lies more than two degrees east of Greenwich!

Blistering barnacles, that's an idea! You may be right! Perhaps we are too far to the west. We'll go back on our tracks...

93

Coxswain at the wheel! ... Helm hard a-port! ... Midships! ... Steer due east.

?

Captain, what is happening? ... We seem to be turning back.

Yes, Professor Calculus, we're turning back.

Oh, that's all right then ... I was afraid we were turning back.

How easy it is to be mistaken. I'd have sworn we'd turned back.

That evening...

There it is at last! Our treasure island!

It's too late to go ashore tonight. We'll drop anchor, and tomorrow we'll explore the island ...

Right! ...

Next morning ...

Haul the boat up the beach. I'm going to reconnoitre

BANG

Crumbs! What's happened to him?

Captain, what was it? Are you hurt?

No. I stubbed my toe against that thing and fell over. That's how the gun went off...

OW! OW!

keep calm! keep calm!
YOW!

Here...

YEOW!

YOW!
YEOW!

Oh, leave them... Come and help me dig up this piece of wood. It intrigues me.

Hello, what have they found?

These are the remains of the jolly-boat in which Sir Francis Haddock once came ashore on this island...

This certainly proves that we're nearing our goal. Red Rackham's treasure is out there at the bottom of the sea!... But now, shoes on, everyone, and let's carry on!

WOOAH!

That's Snowy!... He ran on ahead!...

? !

Where did you get that bone from Snowy?... Here, show us where you found it.

Blistering barnacles! I bet these are the remains of the pirates killed when the UNICORN blew up!

They can't be, Captain.

If they were, we'd have found them down by the shore. No, look at this spear. It's more likely that they were natives, killed in a fight, and probably eaten on the spot by their enemies.

Eaten?... Do you mean cannibals lived on this island?... Man-eaters?

That's what we're going to find out. Come on.

Ouch! I've got a pebble in my shoe!

You go on. I'll catch you up...

Look!... There!...

An idol!...

Yes, an idol... But... It's incredible

My word! It's meant to be Sir Francis Haddock!

Look at that mouth! His voice must have made an enormous impression on the natives. I can just imagine their faces the first time they heard him shout: "Ration my rum!"

RRRATION MY RRRUM!

What's the matter, Captain?

Who shouted like that?

What?... Wasn't it you?

No, it wasn't me! Thundering typhoons!

Yes, it's Sir Francis Haddock.

RRRATION MY RRRUM!

It came from over there.

Not a soul!

This island is h-h-haunted, Captain. Let's hurry back t-t-to the sh-sh-ship.

To b-b-be precise: I-let's hurry back t-t-to the sh-sh-ship.

Pithecanthropus!... Pockmark!...

Pockmark yourself, you gibbering ghost!

That's done it!... They've dropped the gun!... Look, here it comes...

Very smart, weren't you, eh?... Look!... Another inch lower, and that would have been the end of Captain Haddock!

Anyway, all's well that ends well!... Shall we go back now, Captain?... We know the island is uninhabited.

Good idea. Let's go.

Thundering typhoons! I just remembered!

The idol!... Are we going to leave it here?

Next day ...

You've made up your mind?

Yes ... Professor Calculus has explained exactly how his machine works. It'll be all right ...

Stop! ... Just a min-   ute! ...

I forgot to tell you. When you locate the wreck, press the little red button on the left of the instrument panel. That releases a small canister attached underneath the machine. It is full of a substance that gives off thick smoke when it comes into contact with water. That will show us where the wreck lies.

A little red button? ..Right!

No, red! A little red button ... You've got it? Good... Well, goodbye, and good luck!

There he goes: he's dived.

This is fun, eh Snowy?

Golly, what a lot of water!

Let's hope nothing goes wrong ...

Gone long? Why, it's only ten minutes since he dived ...

Hello, what's the matter? ... The engine's stopped ... We aren't moving any more!

?!

Thing's look bad, Snowy! Our propeller is entangled in the weeds!

We'll try and free ourselves by going into reverse . . .

It's no good! The propeller is completely jammed... and the engine has stalled!

Well, Snowy my boy, how do we get out of this?

There's only one thing to do: we'll release the smoke-canister. Then at least they'll know where we are... There, we press the little red button here . . .

That's it...

Look!... Look!... Smoke!... He's found the wreck of the UNICORN!

There, Professor Calculus!... Look!... Smoke!... He's found the wreck!

104

OH!

Captain, look there!... Look!... No, over there! Smoke!...He's found the wreck!

Patience, Snowy!...It won't be long before someone comes to rescue us.

Ahoy there!... Lower the dinghy!... We'll drop a buoy over the spot Tintin has marked.

There's the buoy...

..And there's the underwater viewing instrument.

It worries me a bit that Tintin hasn't come up again...

No, but I was a great sportsman in my youth...

..And that accounts for the athletic figure I still have..

Hm?...

To be quite honest, no... It was mostly walking...

Let's see...

Thundering typhoons!.. It's not the wreck!... It's Tintin!

Wonderful! Quick, let me look...

Oh, Columbus!...The propeller has been fouled by weeds!... How can we save him?

Really, Captain! Your eyes have deceived you! It's not the wreck, it is Tintin. He can't resurface ...

Your confounded contraption! I should never have let him go down!

May drown? Well, he had enough oxygen for two hours. He's got...Let's see ... yes, he has just enough for another ten minutes!

I hope they hurry! It's getting more and more difficult to breathe...

What can we do? How can we save him?

Lower a diver?... No, by the time we'd got one equipped and ready, Tintin would be dead ...

No, I've got an idea. Take the anchor!... The anchor used for mooring the buoy!

The an- chor? What for?...

Of course!... We'll try and hook it on to the submarine. Then we'll pull on the rope until the weeds break...

That's it! Let it down... Lower... lower... lower ... gently ...

An anchor!...They're going to try to hook me. Quick, empty the ballast tanks, that'll help them ...

He's understood. He's emptied the ballast tanks to lighten the submarine...A bit to the left, Captain...Good ... Now, pull!

Ah, they've got it!... I'm saved!... Just in time! I'm suffocating.

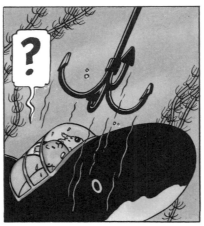

?

Missed!...The anchor hadn't caught properly. Lower it again ... down... stop! A bit to the right...now to the left... Pull it up gently...

Fresh air!... Fresh air at last!...

Hooray!... He's safe!... Hip-hip-hooray!

All's well!... The Captain has climbed back into the boat... He's salvaged the buoy... hauled the anchor inboard... thrown a lifeline to Tintin... Ah, here they come...

Well, our friend Tintin had a narrow escape!

You are wrong, I assure you. Weeds jammed the propeller. You'll see when we're back on board.

You see?... It's just as I said. Weeds...

Really? I thought they were weeds...

Weeds or no weeds, I don't set foot in that thing again!...

Fine. Get it ready. Snowy and I are setting out again immediately!

Let's hope he doesn't run into any more trouble this time.

What shall I do? Tell him ...or not?

I've made up my mind...

I... Captain... I've bad news for you.

Bad news for me?

No, bad news for you, very bad news...I'm afraid the UNICORN is not here... Look...

What's that gadget, eh?

Yes, it's a pendulum. I've taken up the study of divining, and I've arrived at the conclusion I just gave you...

All from that whatsit?

Yes, much further west ...You'll see. My pendulum will begin swinging from east to west... Look, it's started ...

You see?... It's swinging westwards. The UNICORN will be found in that direction.

Look there, Captain! Smoke!

And look, there's the submarine surfacing!.. This time we've got it! ...He's found the wreck!

Have you found it?

Westwards... It's still westwards

Yes, I've found the UNICORN!... You can prepare the diving equipment!

You're sure you'll be all right? ...

Certain! I'll do everything exactly as you told me ..

Good! Now, don't forget... If you want to come up, jerk the line twice... In an emergency, give a series of quick jerks.

Right!

Come on, pump hard!   We are!

?

Wooah! Wooah!

Wooah! Wooah!

Crumbs! What's happening? The air supply has stopped!...

Thundering typhoons! What are you two doing there, instead of pumping?

Us? We're resting...it's tiring work, you know.

You infernal impersonations of Abominable Snowmen! Pump for your lives!...Faster!

Whew!...That's better!...Now the air's coming again. That gave me quite a fright...

Excuse me, Captain, but I don't understand...Since the UNICORN is not here, why has Tintin gone down?

He's picking daisies down below!

?

Having a row? I don't see a boat?

Two jerks on the line! He wants to come up. I'm sure he must have found something!

Heave-ho!...Heave-ho!

Here he is

What has he got?

A gold cross, encrusted with precious stones!...and a cutlass!...I say, this cross is superb!

We've made a good start, eh?

Now why did he tell me that Tintin had gone for a row?

Yes, it's a good start. But this is nothing to what else we shall find. You'll see. I'm going down myself, this time.

By the way... er...any sign of sharks?

No, none at all.

Here's your helmet.

Good.

OW!... OOH! ... OW!

Whatever's the matter?

Blistering barnacles! My beard!

!

There, now your beard is inside.

Good. You can close my helmet now. Keep an eye on that pumping.

Aha! Now to find the treasure!...

A few minutes later...

A series of jerks!... The danger signal!...

Hurry! hurry! pull him up! ... Something frightful must have happened!

Let's hope that it's not a shark...

At last!

A bottle? What can that mean? ...

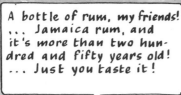

A bottle of rum, my friends! ... Jamaica rum, and it's more than two hundred and fifty years old! ... Just you taste it!

GLUG GLUG GLUG

GLUG GLUG GLUG

Mm! ... It's wonderful ! ... It's absolutely w-w-wonderful ! Y-y-you taste it ! ... Yes, yes, that's f-f-for you! .. I'm g-g-going st-st-st-straight back to g-get a-a-a-another f-for m-myself...

That beats everything! He's gone in without his helmet!

Billions of bilious blue blistering barnacles ! Those two jelly-fishes forgot to pump again ! ...

Sea-gherkins! ... Freshwater swabs! .. Ectoplasms! ... Bashi-bazouks! ...

But ... but it wasn't us, you ...

Silence! You were told to pump, then pump, by thunder!

It's no use drying yourself, Captain. You must empty your suit first ... Take it off now.

Take it off ? ... Never ! ... Never ! ...

I'll rest a minute, and go down again ...

114

He's grabbed the casket!

Goodness, he's swallowed it! And he's coming back for me!

He's coming again. What can I do? If only I had a weapon.

Perhaps this bottle will help...

Quick, back against this old rib. Then he won't sever my air-pipe...

116

Good heavens, what a blow!

Thank goodness my suit isn't damaged.

?

My stars! He's drunk!

Now he's sleeping it off, I suppose. Here's my chance to try and recover the casket.

Two jerks on the line! He wants us to pull him up.

Heave-ho!... Heave-ho!... You wait! He'll be bringing us the treasure.

Thundering typhoons! Why does he have to struggle so?

?

Blistering barnacles, a shark! What a fellow; he's caught a shark!... But what does he want us to do with it?

The best thing is to ask him.

Of course!... Lower another line to him, and pull him up.

Now, up I go I wonder what the Captain will say!

117

That's it!... I've got it!

These are old documents!... Definitely!... Old documents!

That chap will drive me crazy!

And you there? Thundering typhoons, what are you doing?

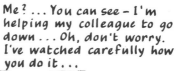
Me?... You can see – I'm helping my colleague to go down... Oh, don't worry. I've watched carefully how you do it...

What about the pump? The pump works by itself, I suppose?

I'll work the pump, nincompoop!... Then at least I'll know he's safe.

Thundering typhoons! What's that over there, on the deck?

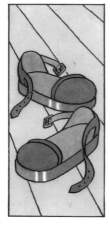
The weighted boots!... He's forgotten the weighted boots!

A fortnight later...
Here we are, pumping as usual...
As usual...

Blistering barnacles! You can stop pumping! Can't you see that Tintin's come up?

Well?
Nothing... Nothing at all! I've been carefully through all that's left of the poop...

It's just as I said: we aren't going to find it.
Come on, Captain, you ...

Tell me, what is that cross over there?

A cross? Where can you see a cross?

No, a cross... that cross over there on the is- land.

It certainly is a cross, isn't it? ...

I say, Captain, Professor Calculus is right! There is a cross, over on the tip of the island!

A cross?

You think so?

Thundering typhoons! It is indeed a cross!

Really? I'd have sworn it was a cross!

Hooray!... Hip-hip-hip-hooray!... I've got it!

?

Professor Calculus, Professor Calculus, you've saved us!

Let me waltz ♪♪ with you ♫♫, The whole ♪♪ night through ♫♫

Quickly, Captain!... Picks!... Shovels!... We're going back to the island.

Yes, Captain, the treasure lies there! You remember the words in Sir Francis Haddock's message: "then shines forth the Eagle's cross". There it is: the Eagle's cross!

Thundering typhoons! You're right!

Hooray! Thomson! ...Thompson! ...Fetch the picks and shovels! Hurry up!...Into the dinghy!

Well, Professor Calculus, we can never thank you enough!

It is rather rough..

No, I said it is thanks to you that we are going to find the treasure.

Oh... Well, I'm sure it's a cross!

Of course, of course it is a cross..

No?... D'you think so?

Baboon! Fresh-water swab!

Hello, my old friend!

Hooray! Here it is!

Gentlemen, this is it, the Eagle's cross!

Well, what did I tell you? Is it or is it not a cross?

Why, what's the meaning of all these notches?

A calendar! When your ancestor was marooned like Robinson Crusoe, he counted the days until he was rescued. Look: there's a small notch for weekdays, and a large one for Sundays...

To work, to work! I'll give a bottle of rum to whoever finds the treasure!

Are you... er... looking for something?...

!

Blistering barnacles, put away your pendulum; come and give us a hand instead!

Towards the west; yes, it does...

What can they be searching for like that?

But... no, it's impossible!

What?... What is so impossible?

That the treasure can be here!

W-w-what?... Why?...

Just think... Supposing Sir Francis Haddock left the UNICORN, carrying the treasure; why would he have buried it here, at the foot of this cross?... What would you have done in his place? On the day you left this island you'd have taken the treasure with you, wouldn't you?

But then...

Then?... Probably the treasure is still out there, under the sea!... And we've followed a false trail!

All because of that creature Calculus, blis-tering barnacles!

Yes, it's all your fault, you certified ignoramus!

Yes; I'm tired of telling you: it's further westwards!

Westwards!... Westwards!... I'll give you westwards!

OH!

Now your infernal pendulum's gone west, you Olympic athlete, you!

Wooah! Wooah!

Take that!... And that!... Now it's buried, pestilential pendulum!

There!... And don't mention it again! Come on now, we're going back!

He's furious!

122

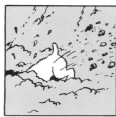

What a good little doggie you are!...

Down, Snowy!...No more games, now!

Is something bothering the Captain?...He seems to be rather worried!

Where have the Siamese twins got to?

Why, I thought they were behind us.

AHOY! THOMSON! THOMPSON!

No, no, please don't worry. The little dog brought it back for me.

Billions of blue blistering barnacles! This time I've had enough!

Captain! Captain!

Leave me alone! I've got to let fly at something!

Thousands of thundering typhoons! That's the lot, eh?

125

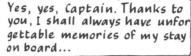

Look, Mr. Calculus, I don't quite follow...

Of course! But let me give you a little advice: don't tell anyone!

And you may rely on me — I will keep this strictly between ourselves!

Well, Captain, our mission is completed. Because he knew we were aboard, Max Bird didn't dare interfere with your activities.

No doubt... You're going home now?

No, we're a bit tired... The journey, you know... and the pumping... We're going to spend a few days in the country with a farmer friend of ours.

Have a good holi -day!

Now for the simple, healthy tasks of the countryside! No more pumping!

To be precise: no more pumping!

... and when you've finished crushing the oats, you can have a turn at the chaff-cutter.

Some days later...

RRRRING

Good morning, Tintin.

Hello, Professor Calculus. What brings you here?

Very well, thank you. And you?... I've come to bring you the documents...

The documents?... What documents?...

No, the documents we found in the casket... Don't you remember?... I've tried to piece them together, sticking the fragments on sheets of paper. Some are illegible. Others, like that one, are comparatively easy to decipher.

I believe that one will interest the Captain particularly.

Great snakes! I think so too!

Come on! We must see the Captain!

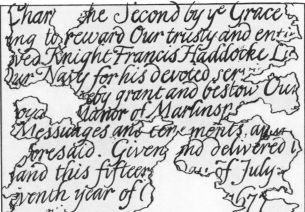

That's all right! I have some money.

You?... You've got money?... That's nice for you!... Personally, I haven't any!

Quite! The government have paid me a large sum for the patent on my submarine. Thanks to you I was able to try it out. Now it's my turn to help you... Come along, we're going to buy your mans— ion.

HOUSE FOR SALE

This HOUSE is not FOR S.LE Haddock

All's well that ends well! ...You haven't found the treasure, but you have got back your family estate.

It is magnificent!

Wait, you haven't seen anything yet.

This is the room where I telephoned you.

Splendid!

SSH!

No...Nothing...I thought I heard footsteps...

Oh?

Well, it's a wonderful house! ... My ancestor had good taste, didn't he?...Now what about those famous cellars you talked of? Where are they?

Come with me... I'll take you there.

Look! Here we are!

Thundering typhoons!

What a lot of junk!... All this junk!

Oh yes, the Bird brothers used this as a storeroom.

Look, that's St. John the Evangelist. We must be in an old chapel...

What do you think of it?

Incre- dible!

Sh!... This time I'm sure I heard a noise...!

It's gone... The footsteps have stopped... It's queer. I wonder...

What?

Why, whatever's the matter? What is it?

Hooray!

The Eagle's cross!... "And then shines forth the Eagle's cross"! There it is... the Eagle's cross...

The Eagle's cross?... I can see a cross, but where is the Eagle?

There, in front of you!

Yes there, look!... St. John the Evangelist – who is always depicted with an eagle... And he's called the Eagle of Patmos – after the island where he wrote his Revelation... He's the Eagle!...

There's a globe!

And an eagle!... You're right! ...

There, just on the spot given in the old parchment, is the island we went to!... Great snakes! The island's moving!

?

!?

*⑥!?

The treasure!... The treasure!!... Blistering treasures! It's Red Rackham's barnacles!

We've found it!... We've found it at last: Red Rackham's treasure!... Look!... Look!

It's stupendous!...Stupendous!...So Sir Francis Haddock did take the treasure with him when he left the UNICORN...And to think we were looking for it half across the world, when all the time it was lying here, right under our very noses...

Thundering typhoons, look at this!...Diamonds!... Pearls!...Emeralds!...Rubies! ...Er...all sorts!...They're magnificent!

Sh!... Did you hear that?

Yes...

Listen... Footsteps! ...Someone's coming towards the cellars ...

Quick! Get hold of a weapon! We'll each hide behind a pillar...

Right! Come on!

POSTSCRIPT

The Secret of the Unicorn and *Red Rackham's Treasure*, the eleventh and twelfth books in *The Adventures of Tintin* were first published in Belgium in 1942 and 1943.

The war had put an end to the journal *XXème siècle*, and with it to the children's supplement *Le Petit Vingtième*, where, until 1940, Hergé had published all his strips. On 11 June 1942 an announcement appeared in the leading Brussels daily *Le Soir* that their supplement, *Soir Jeunesse*, was that day starting publication of a new Tintin adventure, *The Secret of the Unicorn*.

In earlier days *The Adventures of Tintin* had been published weekly, with two pages appearing at a time. In *Soir Jeunesse* the strip appeared daily, forcing Hergé into a new style and a new rhythm. He was restricted to three or four frames each day, with the need to keep the reader in suspense at the end of every line, not just at the end of a page. Looking at these two books with this in mind, the number of jokes, surprises and dramas is astonishing.

At the same time that a change of journal forced Hergé to transform his work, the style of publication of the adventures in book form was profoundly altered. Before the war, the number of pages in *The Adventures of Tintin* varied from book to book. Some had just over 100 pages, others as many as 130. The increasingly severe paper restrictions brought about by the war curtailed Hergé's freedom. Casterman, Hergé's publishers, had to reduce the number of pages. In future, each book must fit into the narrow confines of 62 pages. But there was also a gain. For the first time *The Adventures of Tintin* were printed in colour. The first of the new-style books was *The Shooting Star*, in 1942. The second, a year later, was *The Secret of the Unicorn*.

The Secret of the Unicorn appeared in *Le Soir* from 11 June 1942 to 14 January 1943 at the rate of one strip each day. In all, a total of 174 strips were published. *Red Rackham's Treasure* quickly followed and was published in the same way from 19 February to 23 September 1943, with 183 strips in all.

The front page of *Le Soir* for 11 June 1942, the day on which publication of *The Secret of the Unicorn* began. Through an astonishing misprint the famous detectives, in French Dupond and Dupont, are referred to as Durand and Durant.

'TODAY
The new extraordinary adventures of
TINTIN AND MILOU
with the CAPTAIN
the detectives Durand-Durant
and all the gang.'

PETITE GAZETTE

CAMP VOLANT

Je vous parlais hier de Tessenderloo et du voyage que j'y fis en la compagnie des Volontaires du Travail. A la vérité, l'équipe du Chantier-Ecole se trouve déjà sur les lieux depuis le 10 mai; les autres camps du Service des V. T. de Wallonie auront à fournir (ou ont fourni déjà) quelques journées de travail en cette région du pays. C'est ainsi que je quittai Bruxelles, l'autre matin, en camion, avec l'équipe des Meneurs de Jeu, installée à Uccle, et les Volontaires du Centre.

Il fallait voir la belle humeur qui présidait à ce voyage, tandis que le camion, actionné au gaz à bois, s'engageait, soufflant, peinant, crachotant, sur les routes brabançonnes. Ces jeunes gens, habitués à une vie rude et saine au plein air, ne cessaient de chanter tout le long du chemin comme si, par la seule vertu de leur chant, le moteur eut à fournir le rendement nécessaire. Belles chansons de nos pays de Flandre et de Wallonie, et ces vieux airs français dont la gentillesse et la naïveté, la truculence aussi, raniment l'esprit et

Aujourd'hui

LES NOUVELLES AVENTURES
EXTRAORDINAIRES DE

TINTIN ET MILOU

avec le CAPITAINE,
les détectives Durand-Durant
et toute la troupe.

POUR NOS PRISONNIERS
DE GUERRE

DE LA CELLULOSE
DANS LA MANGEOIRE

Désormais les vaches et les chevaux mangeront de la colle et de la cellulose. Le bois, qui au temps des grandes découvertes techniques et chimiques, nous avait réservé maintes surprises, est devenu maintenant un principe important de la science de la nutrition humaine et animale. A l'heure actuelle, il occupe une place de premier plan dans la production de la viande. Depuis que la science a percé le mystère de la structure des cellules du bois et a constaté dans la cellulose, la présence du sucre et de l'hydrate de carbone, comme éléments essentiels provenant du bois, on n'abandonnait pas l'idée d'employer ces matières comme produits alimentaires et fourragers. En effet, le sucre et l'hydrate de carbone sont des matières qu'on donne aux animaux ensemble avec d'autres aliments, comme par exemple, les pommes de terre les navets, l'avoine et d'autres produits ba-

LES AVENTURES EXTRAORDINAIRES
DE TINTIN ET MILOU
TEXTES ET DESSINS DE
...HERGÉ

above   The opening strip of *The Secret of the Unicorn* from *Le Soir*. The pictures from the newspaper were slightly altered when they later appeared in the books.

centre   The closing strip of *The Secret of the Unicorn*. Tintin and Captain Haddock do not announce publication of *Red Rackham's Treasure* but the serial 'Juck and Jimbo learn history' which will fill the gap in the newspaper.

below   The opening strip of *Red Rackham's Treasure*.

LES AVENTURES DE TINTIN ET MILOU
TEXTE ET DESSINS DE HERGÉ

A SEARCH FOR TREASURE

The two books, although written during the war, are works of pure escapism. Almost alone among Hergé's stories they are untouched by the realities of the times. To Hergé, *The Secret of the Unicorn* is the favourite among his books.

In taking a treasure-hunt for his subject, Hergé uses a classic theme in a highly personal way. Particularly, he gives great importance to a period frequently overlooked by the story-tellers: preparation for the voyage. Hergé devotes a whole book to this, with a brilliantly original narrative. In his writing he draws together three separate strands to achieve his ends, just as, to discover the position of the *Unicorn*, the three parchments must be superimposed.

The first strand, the most obvious, is the patient search by Tintin and Captain Haddock for the three models of the *Unicorn*, and their battle of wits with the other treasure-hunters, the mysterious Ivan Ivanovitch Sakharine, and more importantly, the formidable Bird brothers.

The second strand, which only joins the main thread at the very last moment, is the hunt for stolen wallets by the twin detectives, the Thompsons (who acquit themselves with all their usual brilliance). Once the thief has been caught, Tintin finds two of the precious parchments in one of the wallets.

The third element, and the most original, is Captain Haddock's re-creation of the exploits of his seventeenth-century ancestor, Sir Francis Haddock. Captain Haddock's part here is of entirely unsuspected importance, and certainly one of the most significant aspects of *The Secret of the Unicorn* is the confirmation of the Captain as Tintin's friend.

Emerging as a somewhat colourless figure in *The Crab with the Golden Claws*, a drunken captain bossed by a scheming mate, Allan, Captain Haddock achieves greater substance in *The Shooting Star*, where he emerges as a real personality, master of the expedition's ship *Aurora*.

It is in *The Secret of the Unicorn* that Captain Haddock attains his full stature, with a unique historical dimension. The Captain is the only character in the series who is given origins, who has a past. The contrast is striking between the Captain and Tintin, the hero. Tintin has no family, his age is uncertain, and he has no real job. Captain Haddock has an ancestor: and what an ancestor! Fierce and full-blooded, he anticipates by three hundred years the vocabulary of his future descendant.

CAPTAIN HADDOCK'S 'FAMILY'

While the Captain's fictional ancestor is a creation of Hergé's brilliant imagination, it is nonetheless true that by extraordinary coincidence several real sailors by the name of Haddock have been found.

In England, at Leigh on Sea, a family named Haddock recorded several captains in their time, and an admiral, Richard Haddock, almost an exact contemporary of Sir Francis Haddock since he lived from 1629 to 1715. Inside the church at Leigh on Sea are family memorials, among which is a record of the exploits of Sir Richard Haddock, commander of the *Royal James*, flagship of the Earl of Sandwich at the Battle of Sole Bay. When his ship was set on fire and every effort to save her failed, the admiral cast himself into the sea in a gesture worthy of his Hergéan namesake. Luckily for him he was saved from the water, and after the rescue was presented to the king, Charles II. To restore the admiral's spirits the king removed his own satin cap and placed it upon Sir Richard's head.

A totem representing Sir Francis Haddock.

Another Captain Haddock was brought to Hergé's notice in 1961. His story is perhaps less distinguished than that of the admiral, but is still not unrelated to his imaginary namesake. This second Captain Haddock is known through his trial before an Admiralty board in 1674. The captain was in command of the fireship *Anne and Christopher* in the Mediterranean. Having lost his squadron, he put into port for several days and took aboard goods which he sold in England upon his return, not forgetting to levy his commission. Sentence pronounced at the end of the trial was light: Haddock was ordered to forfeit all profits from his unwarlike activities and was suspended from his command for six months.

Finally, on 22 July 1963 the Montreal daily *La Presse* published an article referring to a contemporary Captain Haddock. The story related to a collision at sea between two ships, the *Roonagh Head* and the *Tritonica*. The captain of the *Roonagh Head* was none other than

A portrait of Sir Francis Haddock painted by Jacques Laudy from Hergé's drawings.

W A Haddock (A for Archibald, perhaps, which is, as readers of *Tintin and the Picaros* will know, the Captain's christian name). Aged 61, this other Captain Haddock was commodore of the Head Line, a holder of the OBE for distinguished services in the Second World War, when he worked in espionage with Allied agents.

Hergé knew nothing of these other mariners when, in 1940, he created his own Captain Haddock, whose immense importance to the series he could not then foresee.

THE REAL RED RACKHAM

If, as in the case of Captain Haddock's origins, fact has, so to speak, caught up with fiction, there are other instances where Hergé was willingly influenced by events and by real people.

Red Rackham the pirate, however romantic he may seem, was based upon a real character. Just as he introduced Al Capone in person in *Tintin in America*, and in *The Broken Ear* clearly portrayed as Bazil Bazaroff the arms dealer Bazil Zaharoff, Hergé cheerfully transported the pirate Jean Rackham more or less complete into his book.

Jean Rackham began his career with an exploit worthy of his fictional counterpart. In about 1718 (a little after the date of Hergé's story) Rackham was quartermaster of the ship commanded by the famous pirate Charles Vane. One day, Vane's ship spotted a French vessel; at first sight it appeared to be of small account, but having taken stock of the newcomer's armaments Vane decided that his best course was to turn tail and avoid an encounter. Rackham, on the other hand, argued that this was faint-hearted counsel; to board the ship would bring rich rewards.

The ship's company was divided. Fifteen or sixteen supported Vane; the rest preferred to chance their luck with Rackham. But the laws of piracy were strict: in the face of the enemy the captain's word was absolute. The pirate ship beat a hasty retreat.

Next day the crew gave vent to their bitterness. Charles Vane was accused of cowardice, relieved of his command, and set adrift in a boat with the sailors who had taken his part. The rest of the company set course for the Caribbean under their new captain, Jean Rackham. For two years Rackham sailed in triumph, spreading terror across the seas. But on 1 November 1720, towards six o'clock in the evening, the pirate met his destiny. Surprised by another vessel, Rackham gave fight. This time, however, he misjudged the enemy. His defeat was swift and final. The hapless Rackham was caught and tried, and sentenced to the gallows.

THE HISTORY OF THE 'UNICORN'

Hergé is often asked about the origins of the ships portrayed in the two books, and particularly the most famous of all, the *Unicorn*. The exactness of the drawing is such that invention alone could not suffice. As always with Hergé, a great deal of meticulous research and documentation took place before he made a start. The *Unicorn* is not an exact portrayal of a single ship. Hergé was inspired by the drawings of a number of different vessels he saw in the Musée de la Marine in Paris. From there he drew together all the details he needed to create his own particular ship.

As he has drawn her, *Unicorn* is remarkably faithful to the characteristics of the French navy in the seventeenth century. French ships were divided into five classes rated according to their fire-power. A careful study of Hergé's drawings reveals fifty guns aboard the ship commanded by Sir Francis Haddock. According to the conventions of that time she would have been classed as a third-rate vessel, something over 40 metres long and about 11 metres broad.

Each of the cannon carried by such a ship weighed about three tons; it took a dozen men to manoeuvre one of them. The size of the crew was therefore more or less determined: two hundred men at least to man the guns, with the whole crew in time of war totalling about three hundred and fifty.

Hergé's principal model was undoubtedly *Le Brillant*, built at Le Havre in 1690 by the master-carpenter Salicon. Hergé took

The stern of the *Soleil Royal*, one of the ships that inspired Hergé in his creation of the *Unicorn*.

from the ship all the essentials of the decoration created by the sculptor Jean Berain who had been charged by Louis XIV with the task of co-ordinating all naval design.

Only the unicorn on the prow does not belong to the *Brillant*. No French ship has borne that name, and the figurehead, with its magical associations, was probably suggested to Hergé by the famous British frigate *Unicorn*, built in 1745.

over Plan of the *Unicorn* drawn shortly after World War II by G. Liger-Belair.

Model of the Danish vessel *Enhjornigen* (*Unicorn*), presented by publisher Carlsen to Hergé during a visit to Copenhagen.

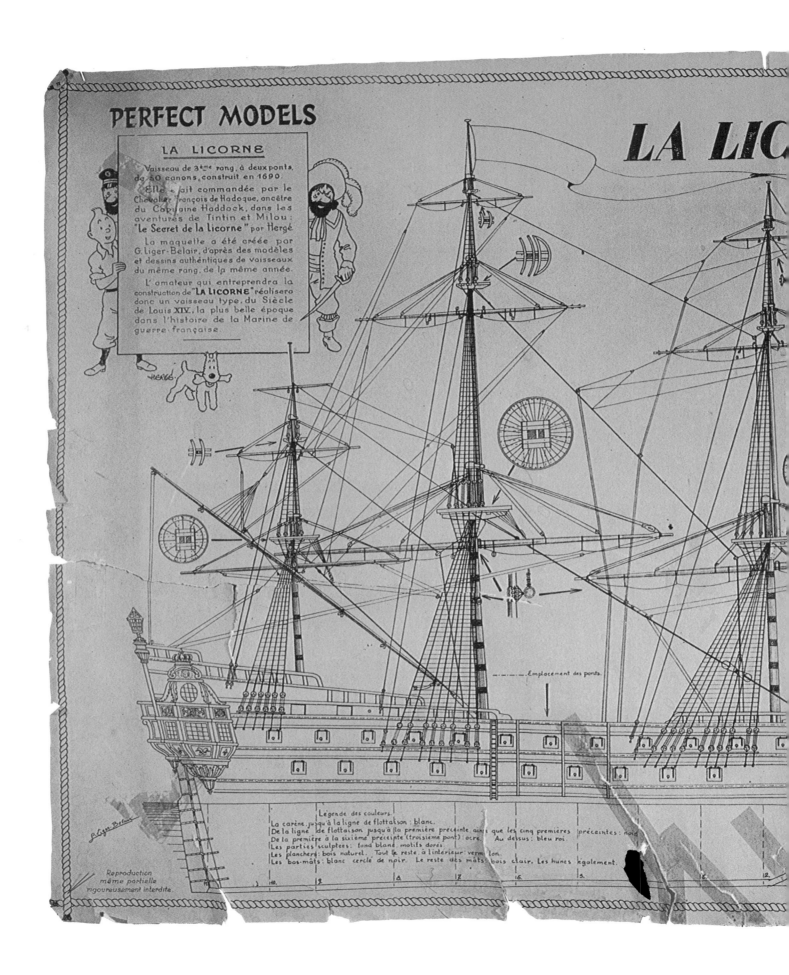

PERFECT MODELS

LA LICORNE

Vaisseau de 3ème rang, à deux ponts, de 50 canons, construit en 1690.

Elle a été commandée par le Chevalier François de Hadoque, ancêtre du Capitaine Haddock, dans les aventures de Tintin et Milou: "Le Secret de la Licorne" par Hergé.

La maquette a été créée par G. Liger-Belair, d'après des modèles et dessins authentiques de vaisseaux du même rang, de la même année.

L'amateur qui entreprendra la construction de "LA LICORNE" réalisera donc un vaisseau type, du Siècle de Louis XIV, la plus belle époque dans l'histoire de la Marine de guerre française.

HERGÉ

LA LIC

.......Emplacement des ponts.

Légende des couleurs.
La carène jusqu'à la ligne de flottaison: blanc.
De la ligne de flottaison jusqu'à la première préceinte ainsi que les cinq premières préceintes: noir.
De la première à la sixième préceinte (troisième pont): ocre. Au dessus: bleu roi.
Les parties sculptées: fond blanc, motifs dorés.
Les planchers: bois naturel. Tout le reste à l'intérieur: vermillon.
Les bas-mâts: blanc cerclé de noir. Le reste des mâts: bois clair. Les hunes également.

G. Liger-Belair

142

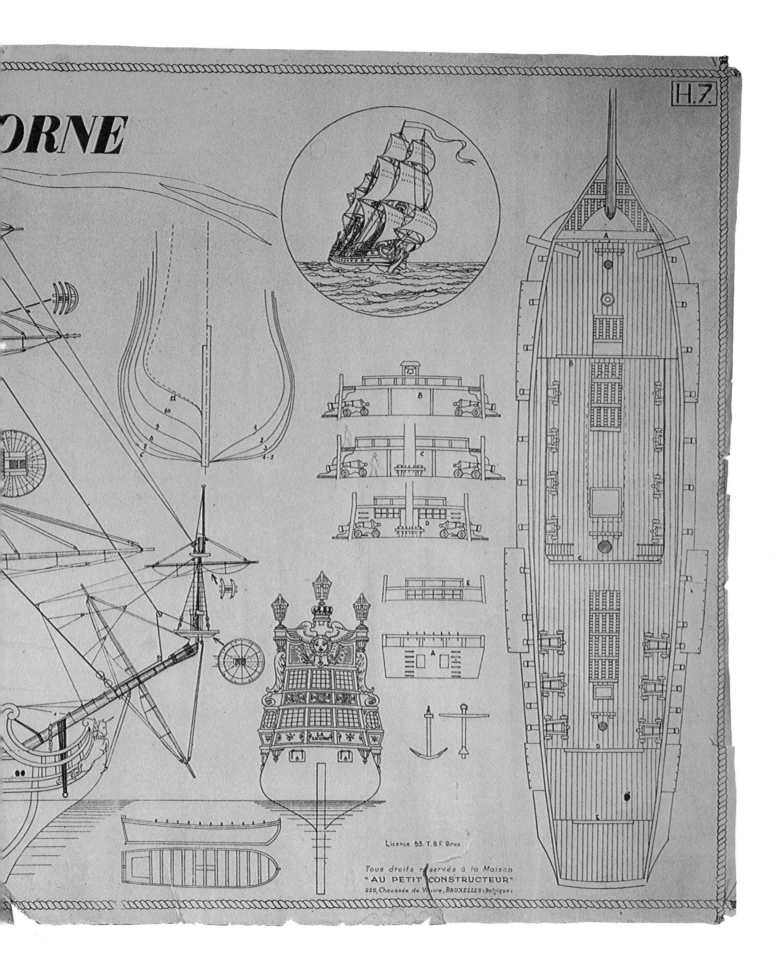

LORNE

H.7.

A SCALE MODEL OF THE 'UNICORN'

The vessel *Unicorn* designed by Hergé, inspired by a number of actual ships, has in its turn become the pattern for many other re-creations, the most remarkable of which is certainly the model built by a passionate admirer of Hergé, Jean-Claude Lemineur.

In 1976 Monsieur Lemineur, a Belgian architect, began the fulfilment of one of his childhood dreams: to construct a scale model of the *Unicorn*. Not content to build an ordinary model, Lemineur began an extraordinary piece of research which led him not only to the sources used by Hergé but also to much detail concerning the French navy of the period. (It is from Monsieur Lemineur that much of the naval information used here is derived.)

His model, scale 1:48, is 1.15 metres long and is entirely made from original materials fashioned piece by piece; it is the work of a craftsman. Each of the guns, made from a lead-tin-antimony alloy, was separately cast in a plaster mould before being mounted and painted bronze. All the ship's ornament was carved in lime (chosen for its even texture) and delicately decorated with gold leaf.

Construction of the model to its present stage has occupied more than 2,500 hours over a period of six years, and will take its creator a further 1,500 hours to complete. Even now it represents one of the most remarkable and beautiful pieces of work inspired by the world of Hergé.

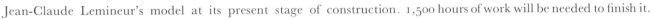

Jean-Claude Lemineur's model at its present stage of construction. 1,500 hours of work will be needed to finish it.

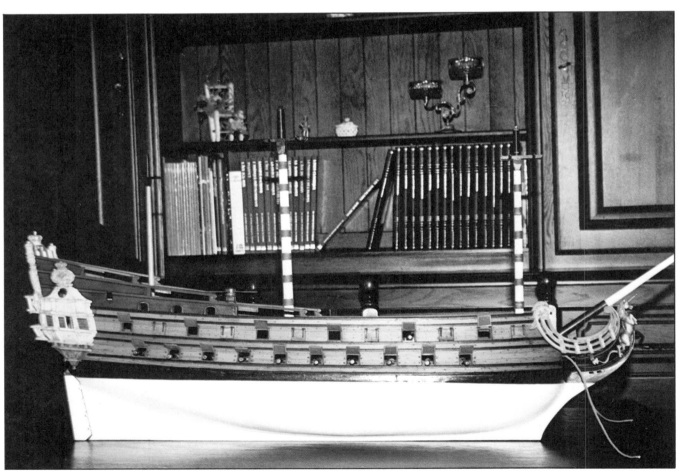

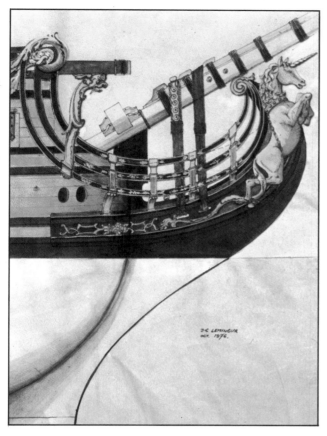

above left . Preliminary sketch for construction of the model.

above right   Figurehead for the model of the *Unicorn*.

below right   The miniature cannon ranged for battle.

below left   Stages in the modelling of a cannon: casting, trimming, painting.

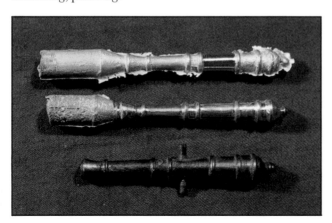

A RECONSTRUCTION IN THREE DIMENSIONS

While the work of Monsieur Lemineur is notable for its precision, another reconstruction is remarkable for its size. In the Walibi amusement park near Brussels is a three-dimensional portrayal of the great sequence from *The Secret of the Unicorn* in which Captain Haddock re-enacts the exploits of his ancestor.

A decision to build the attraction was made in 1978, and from the start the Studios Hergé were closely involved. Hergé's principal collaborator Bob De Moor had visited 'Disneyworld' in Florida and seen one of the principal attractions, 'The pirates of the Caribbean'. On his return he made the preliminary sketches for the transformation of the book.

Housed in a building 60 metres by 40.8 metres high, in the shape of a fortified seventeenth-century château, the Walibi exhibit was opened in the early part of 1980. Visitors see a magnificent animated reconstruction of the battle between the ships of Sir Francis Haddock and Red Rackham. Sitting in a small boat, carried along by water, they follow the principal events of the story to an accompaniment of sea-shanties.

The creation of this remarkable feature, perhaps the forerunner of a future 'Hergéworld', took more than 100,000 hours of work over two years, with two replicas of the *Unicorn* and one of a pirate ship with only a one-third reduction in size, innumerable animated figures in period costume, Tintin, the Captain, Red Rackham and his ruffians, and even the monkeys and the parrots.

Drawing by Bob De Moor of the fortified château housing the feature at Walibi.

Construction of replicas of the *Unicorn*.

Preliminary sketches by Bob De Moor
for the three-dimensional feature.

148

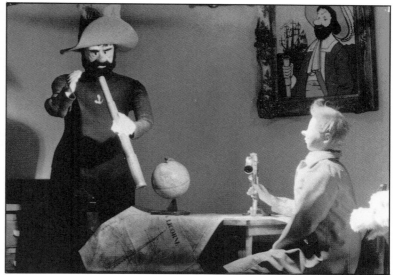

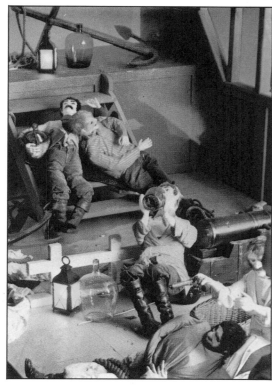

Five scenes from Walibi.

THE COMING OF CUTHBERT CALCULUS

So many jewels are to be found in *The Secret of the Unicorn* that *Red Rackham's Treasure*, the second part of a remarkable tale, might also be overlooked. It is in fact the best-selling of Hergé's books, made up of many elements, with a story in the best traditions of Robert Louis Stevenson and Jules Verne.

However, to the true connoisseur of Hergé's work the greatest significance of *Red Rackham's Treasure* is unquestionably the arrival of Professor Cuthbert Calculus (**Tryphon Tournesol**). It is a marvellous début. All his efforts to go with Tintin and the Captain in their search for treasure are fiercely rebuffed; in the end he is forced to creep aboard the *Sirius* as a stowaway. He seems to be a character trying to get in, with the story determined to keep him out, almost a time of trial before being fully admitted to the series. Captain Haddock in his time underwent a similar probation.

At this critical point in the development of his work Hergé put the finishing touches to his 'family'. Around the neutral figure of Tintin a circle developed with lively, colourful characters who quickly grew out of their secondary roles. To begin with, Tintin and Snowy were alone. They were joined in turn by the Thompsons (les Dupond/ts), the Captain, and now Professor Calculus. With the arrival of the Professor the central group is complete. The only newcomer of importance will be Jolyon Wagg (Séraphin Lampion), first encountered in *The Calculus Affair*, but he remains a lesser figure, never succeeding, despite his efforts, in joining the family circle.

As with so many components of *The Adventures of Tintin* Cuthbert Calculus also had his

Professor Auguste Piccard, Hergé's inspiration for the character of Cuthbert Calculus.

Sous-Marin   Allemagne.

03.02.04.02.05.

9.

Der U-Boot-Zwerg

Ein Amerikaner hat sich ein winziges Unterseeboot kon-
struiert, mit dem er den Michigansee unter Wasser durch-
fahren will. Das Boot hat Fischform und ist mit Periskop
ausgerüstet. In der Regel fährt der Erfinder einen
Meter unter Wasser, er ist aber auch schon bis zu zehn
Meter tief getaucht!   Presse-Photo (2)

A document from the archives at Studios Hergé. The German U-boat probably served as a model for the submarine invented by Professor Calculus.

original. The character was inspired by the famous inventor of the bathyscaphe, Professor Auguste Piccard, who died in 1962.

"In appearance, Tournesol and his submarine are primarily Professor Auguste Piccard and his bathyscaphe. But a scaled-down Piccard, for the original was too large. He had an endless neck which shot up from an oversized collar. I sometimes passed him in the street and he seemed to me the incarnation of a 'savant'. I made Tournesol as a mini-Piccard, otherwise I would have had to enlarge the frames for the drawings." (Hergé, in *Tintin et moi, entretien avec Hergé* by Numa Sadoul, Casterman, 1975.)

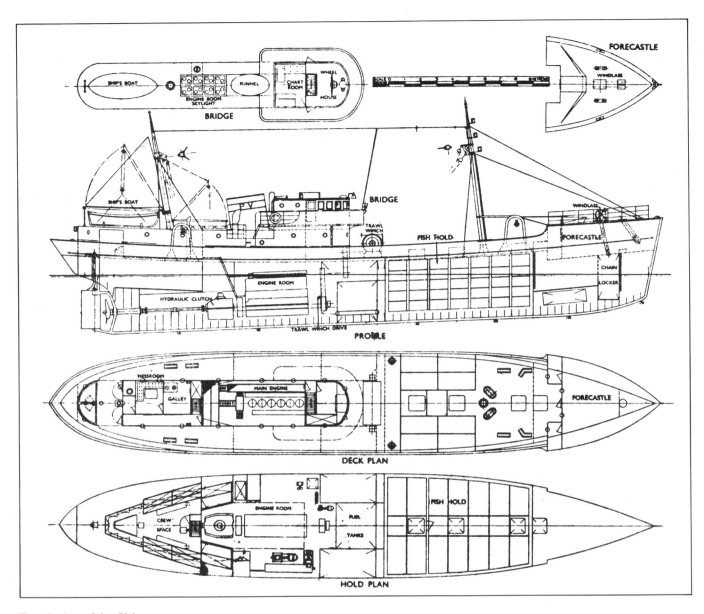

BRIDGE

FORECASTLE

PROFILE

DECK PLAN

HOLD PLAN

Detail plan of the *Sirius*.

opposite   A model of the *Sirius*.

MARLINSPIKE HALL

In addition to Professor Calculus, another fundamental feature is first created in this two-part story: Marlinspike Hall (le château de Moulinsart) with the faithful Nestor, who seems almost a part of the house itself.

The appearance, and then the acquisition of the Haddock family seat brings a major change to *The Adventures of Tintin*. From the small apartments at the beginning of *The Secret of the Unicorn* to the magnificent family mansion is a tremendous step. It means that the characters are no longer homeless. Between adventures they have somewhere to rest (unless of course the Milanese Nightingale invites herself to stay).

Marlinspike was suggested to Hergé by one of the many châteaux of the Loire valley: le château de Cheverny. But it is a Cheverny shorn of its wings as drawn by Hergé, no doubt to make it less pretentious and more suited to modern times. The French name *Moulinsart* is an inversion of a Belgian place-name, *Scarmoulin*.

Many stories attach to Moulinsart. Some years ago a Brussels lawyer enacted the sale. Everything was correctly ordered, and the house was duly purchased by Captain Haddock with money generously given by Professor Calculus. Again, on the outskirts of Brussels a copy of Moulinsart has been built. What greater homage can one pay to an author than to live in the house of his heroes?

The mingling of fact and fiction portrayed in these pages is more than mere anecdote. It demonstrates the power of the books. The world of Hergé has become a part of our reality. He has succeeded in changing the way in which we look at things. Perhaps there is no greater achievement for a work of art.

LES CHÂTEAUX HISTORIQUES DE FRANCE

CHEVERNY

UN DES BEAUX CHÂTEAUX
DE LA
LOIRE

Hergé's inspiration: le château de Cheverny.

above A model of Marlinspike Hall.
below A house near Brussels, clearly inspired by the drawings of Hergé.